friends,

e world of

Geronimo Stilton

THE RODENT'S GAZETTE
EDITORIAL STAFF

Geronimo Stilton
A learned and brainy
mouse; editor of
The Rodent's Gazette

Thea Stilton
Geronimo's sister and
special correspondent at
The Rodent's Gazette

Trap Stilton
An awful joker;
Geronimo's cousin and
owner of the store
Cheap Junk for Less

Benjamin Stilton
A sweet and loving
nine-year-old mouse;
Geronimo's favorite
nephew

THE SUPER CUP
FACE-OFF

Scholastic Inc.

Copyright © 2016 Edizioni Piemme S.p.A. © 2018 Mondadori Libri S.p.A. for PIEMME, Italia. International Rights © Atlantyca S.p.A. English translation © 2022 by Atlantyca S.p.A.

The publisher does not have any control over and does not assume any responsibility for author or third-party websites or their content.

GERONIMO STILTON names, characters, and related indicia are copyright, trademark, and exclusive license of Atlantyca S.p.A. All rights reserved. The moral right of the author has been asserted. Based on an original idea by Elisabetta Dami. geronimostilton.com

Published by Scholastic Inc., *Publishers since 1920*, 557 Broadway, New York, NY 10012. SCHOLASTIC and associated logos are trademarks and/or registered trademarks of Scholastic Inc.

Stilton is the name of a famous English cheese. It is a registered trademark of the Stilton Cheese Makers' Association.

ISBN 978-1-338-80226-9

Text by Geronimo Stilton
Original title *Finale di supercoppa . . . a Topazia!*

Art Director: Iacopo Bruno
Cover by Roberto Ronchi, and Alessandro Muscillo
Graphic Designer: Laura Dal Maso/theWorldofDOT
Illustrations by Danilo Loizedda, Antonio Campo, and Daria Cherchi
Translated by Emily Clement
Special thanks to Becky Herrick
Interior design by Becky James

10 9 8 7 6 5 4 3 2 1   22 23 24 25 26

Printed in the U.S.A.   40
First printing 2022

IMMEDIATELY!

One morning, I **woke up** bursting with energy. I'm usually a bit of a *lazy* mouse, but that morning I jumped out of bed before my **alarm** could even go off.

I was very *excited*. It was the day of the

What a beautiful day!

championship soccer matches in the Mouse

Island Super Cup tournament — and
my two **favorite** teams were in the
finals! Squeak!

Oops, I haven't
introduced myself!
My name is Stilton,
Geronimo Stilton.
I run *The Rodent's
Gazette*, the most
famouse newspaper
on Mouse Island.

*Go, Squeakers!
Go, Turbo Cheese!*

That morning, as I
was saying, my **FUR** was bristling with
excitement. Like everyone in New Mouse
City, I'm a soccer fan, although I must admit
that I'm not really an expert on the sport.
My favorite team in the women's division
is Turbo Cheese, which my sister, Thea,

MY FAVORITE TEAMS!

THE SQUEAKERS

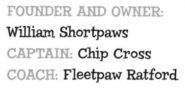

FOUNDER AND OWNER:
William Shortpaws
CAPTAIN: Chip Cross
COACH: Fleetpaw Ratford

TEAM TURBO CHEESE

TURBO CHEESE

FOUNDER AND OWNER:
Bella Ball
CAPTAIN: Hope Goalfur
COACH: Feint van der Foot

plays on. In the men's division, I **cheer** for the Squeakers, which was founded by my grandfather William Shortpaws.

THAT EVENING, BOTH TEAMS I CHEER FOR HAD THE CHANCE TO WIN!

I ran to the newsstand and bought every kind of sports news I could find. Then I went to have **breakfast** at my favorite café, to read all the information and expert opinions

Here's Geronimo Stilton!

Huh?!

I could about the matches.

The teams playing in the **double final** were the Squeakers versus the Mighty Mice and Turbo Cheese versus the Sewer Rats. What I learned was this:

Madame No is the CEO of EGO Corp. (Enormousely Gigantic Organization), a very powerful firm that conducts business of all kinds — even the suspicious kinds! — on Mouse Island. She wants to win, anytime, anywhere, in any way! She has only one answer to any question: "**No!**"

The Mighty Mice and the Sewer Rats were two new teams, both sponsored by Madame No. **Hmm . . . how strange!**

These two teams have each won all their matches up to now. **Hmm . . . how strange!**

Every report agreed that the teams have only won their matches thanks to mysterious accidents happening to their opponents. **Hmm . . . how strange!**

I was nibbling on the last few bits of a cheesy roll when my phone rang.

It was my sister, Thea. "Geronimo! Come to the stadium where I'm practicing with Turbo Cheese right now! Immediately!"

I tried to protest. "But I'm having breakfast and reading the sports pages —"

"Forget breakfast!" Thea squeaked. "We urgently need your help. Something suspicious is happening at the Super Cup, and if we don't find out what's going on, the Squeakers and Turbo Cheese could be cheated out of a win!"

My whiskers trembled with anxiety. "Moldy mozzarella! That would be terrible! I'm coming immediately!"

I hurried to pay . . . but my WALLET slipped out of my paws and coins fell everywhere!

Heeeeelp!

I hurried to the bus . . . but my newspapers started flying away and I had to chase them down!

I got off the bus and hurried toward the stadium . . . but I slipped in a **puddle** and ended up smeared on the ground like cream cheese on a bagel!

Nooooooo!

Argh!

WE ARE SUPER AND YOU ARE NOT!

Finally, I made it into the **STADIUM**. The teams were having their last practices before the finals. The Squeakers and Turbo Cheese shared the field easily and practiced together.

Meanwhile, the Mighty Mice and the Sewer Rats were sprawled in the stands with smug expressions, **GIGGLING** rudely. They were behaving as if they were sure they'd win. They didn't have any doubts!

Hmm . . . how strange!

As **SOON** as she saw me, Thea ran over.

"Thank goodness you're finally here! What are you doing with all those sports pages?" she asked.

"Um . . . I wanted to read up on today's matches, just to learn a little more!"

Thea CHUCKLED. "Forget those — we'll share all the news you need. We know everything about soccer! I'll introduce you to our captain."

Thea turned toward the field and called out, "CAPTAIN!"

An athletic rodent wearing a goalkeeper's uniform and a band on her arm jogged over to us. She had **charming** cornflower-blue eyes and a kind snout.

Geronimo!   It's a pleasure . . .

She politely shook my . "You must be Geronimo! I've heard so much about you from Thea. It's a pleasure to meet you! I'm Hope Goalfur."

"It's a pleasure to meet you," I said, shaking her paw.

Just then my phone rang.

It was CREEPELLA VON CACKLEFUR.

"*Geronimo!* I just had the strangest feeling," she squeaked. "I suddenly found myself missing you a lot!"

"Oh, that's nice to hear," I replied. "We should schedule a time to go out for dinner or a cheese shake. I will have to call you later. I'm very busy!"

"Hmm . . . okay, I can't wait!"

I put away my phone and turned back to

Thea. "So, what's this urgent problem you mentioned?"

Thea lowered her voice. "Geronimo, there's something very, very, very **strange** going on. For some time, mysterious accidents have caused the Mighty Mice and the Sewer Rats to win each of their matches."

Hope nodded. "It's all very **strange**. The other players agree."

The Squeakers' CAPTAIN, Chip Cross, turned toward the field and called out, "Friends! Players! Come here!"

All the players from the Squeakers and Turbo Cheese stopped practicing and ran toward

CHIP CROSS

Chip Cross is the famouse captain of the Squeakers Soccer Club. He's a truly talented player: he's led the Squeakers to win many **Super Cups**. One time, an opposing team even mousenapped him to try to help them win the game!

us, along with the two coaches, Fleetpaw Ratford and Feint van der Foot.

Chip Cross was an old friend of mine and gave me a very big hug. "It's so nice to see you again, Geronimo! It's been way too long! Did you come to **WATCH** us practice?"

I shook my snout. "Thea called me to investigate the **mysterious** accidents at the Mighty Mice's and Sewer Rats' matches."

Those purple spots!

The jerseys . . .

The floating ball . . .

The slippery shoes . . .

A Squeakers player cried, "Yes, it was weird how those jerseys **mysteriously** became so itchy . . ."

A Turbo Cheese player added, "And those **mysteriously** slippery shoes . . ."

Another player squeaked, "And those **mysterious** purple spots . . ."

Another player added, "To say nothing of the **mysterious** floating soccer ball!"

The players all agreed. "When the Mighty Mice and the Sewer Rats play, something always happens to their opponents!"

HMM . . . HOW STRANGE!

Just then I heard a chorus of mean giggles.

The Mighty Mice and Sewer Rats players **heckled** from the stands, "Are you finally done practicing, you slackers?"

"IT'S POINTLESS — YOU'RE ALL GOING TO LOSE ANYWAY!"

Thea replied, "Oh yeah? How are you so sure you're going to win? Do you have some kind of trick in mind?"

The captain of the Sewer Rats **sneered**. "We're sure we'll win because we're better than you, lazyfur!"

Then they walked off, singing,

"We are super and you are not!
We're going to win by an awful lot!"

HUP! HUP! HUP!

Hope Goalfur squealed, "Look! Jim Dribbles is here — he's the most famouse sports announcer on Mouse Island! He's commentated on all the matches in the **TOURNAMENT** so far, so surely he'll have an idea of what's going on!"

The players returned to practice and I rushed over to Jim, who had started JUMPING in place to warm up.

He COMMENTATED on his own actions: "Now the great sportscaster starts his warm-up!

JIM
DRIBBLES

Hup! Hup! Hup! He jumps like a champion!
Hup! Hup! Hup! Look at those muscles go!
Hup! Hup! Hup!"

Then he noticed me and shouted, "And now Jim sees his friend Geronimo Stilton! He approaches! He greets him! Will he hug him? Or won't he? He . . . hugs him!"

I hugged him back. "Hi, Jim! Why are you warming up?"

He went back to jumping in place. "**Hup! Hup! Hup!** I need to be in magnificent shape for the finals tonight! I have to commentate on two matches in a row, and I don't want to miss a beat! **Hup! Hup! Hup!**"

I said, "Oh my — two games in a row seems really **exhausting**. Can't you ask someone to stand in for you?"

"No way!" Jim squeaked. "On my honor as a **SPORTSCASTER**, I'll give it my all and

The DRIBBLES Family

Penalty Dribbles, Jim's grandfather, holds the record for commentating on the most matches ever on Mouse Island. Jim's dream is to break his grandfather's record!

His dad, Kick Dribbles, was a very famouse goalkeeper, with the record for most blocked penalty kicks on Mouse Island.

His mom, Goalanna, was a soccer champion on Mouse Island and holds the record for the fastest goal scored. They called her the Flash!

Ever since he was a mouseling, Jim liked to commentate on his own soccer play!

This was Jim's first time announcing a match! He dedicated it to his grandfather, who taught him everything.

Jim, Geronimo, Thea, and Ola (Jim's sister) have been friends since they were little and have often played soccer together!

do the best announcing possible! **Hup! Hup! Hup!**"

Meanwhile, he was looking at the soccer field where my sister, Thea, was practicing. Ever since he was little, Jim has had a soft spot for Thea. He never wanted her to lose a match!

I said, "Listen, Jim, since you've commentated on the whole championship, what do you think about the **strange** things that have happened during the Mighty Mice's and the Sewer Rats' matches?"

Jim squeaked, "**Hup! Hup! Hup!** You

want to know what I think? Come with me! Let's take a jog. Squeaking while running is part of my sportscaster training!"

I tried to object. "I'm, er, not exactly a sportsmouse . . ."

Thea Stilton

WHO SHE IS: A special correspondent for *The Rodent's Gazette* and Geronimo Stilton's sister.

SPORTS PLAYED: Anything you need to train and practice for! She is particularly good at soccer and is a regular player for the soccer team Turbo Cheese.

HER ADVICE: "Always keep in shape — you never know when it might help you!"

HER PASSION: Other than sports, she loves travel, adventure, and meeting new friends all over the world!

HER MOTTO: "If you dream it, you can do it!"

HER CHILDHOOD DREAM: To spend a weekend in a spaceship and stay overnight on a space station.

But Jim was already *ZIPPING* around the field, saying, "Jim takes off! He runs across the field:

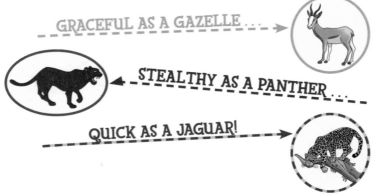

GRACEFUL AS A GAZELLE . . .

STEALTHY AS A PANTHER . . .

QUICK AS A JAGUAR!

"He's leaving Geronimo behind! Uh-oh, if Geronimo doesn't catch up, they won't be able to squeak!"

Rancid ricotta!

Wait!

I dragged myself **behind** him, my tongue hanging out of my mouth. "Aghhh! Rancid ricotta! Wait!"

Jim CHUCKLED and kept commentating. "Geronimo tries to catch up with Jim! But he won't make it! He's too much of a **slowpoke**! The distance between them gets bigger!"

I was trying my best, but I was as

SLOW AS A SLOTH! - - -

Geronimo . . . won't make it!

HOW TO TRAIN TO BE A PERFECT TV SPORTSCASTER

She sells seashells . . .

Stretch while saying tongue twisters to practice staying focused on what you're saying even in stressful situations!

He's out of breath!

La, la, la . . .

Sing a song while running to practice not losing your breath!

Then take a little break and drink water to stay hydrated.

Luckily, once he did a lap around the field, Jim stopped running and went back to **JUMPING** in place while squeaking at the top of his lungs, "**Hup! Hup! Hup!**"

When I finally reached him, worn out, I collapsed. "**Aaagh . . .**" Then I gasped out, "So, tell me what you think about the **strange** things that have happened during the Mighty Mice's and the Sewer Rats' matches."

Jim started doing leg stretches. "I think something **suspicious** is going on! And I'm not the only one. The IRFS has its suspicions, too. In fact, they've hired the most

IRFS

INTERNATIONAL RODENT FEDERATION OF SOCCER

This international organization regulates matches between rodent soccer teams at all levels, for all ages, on Mouse Island.

famouse referee on Mouse Island, Sharp Foulfur, to referee the match."

I let out a sigh of relief. "Then everything will be okay. Sharp is famouse for his **honesty**!"

Jim bent down to do push-ups. "Mm-hmm, that's great, but we still have to watch very, very carefully! Something **suspicious** is going on."

I agreed. "You're right, Jim. We'd better keep our eyes open. I don't trust *Madame No*. She has no morals, and she just wants to win — anytime, anywhere, in any way! Who knows what she's come up with this time!"

Then I exclaimed, "I'M GOING TO CALL ALL MY FRIENDS RIGHT AWAY. Together we'll figure out what to do."

Geronimo
Volunteers!

A little later, just in time for lunch, we all met back at *The Rodent's Gazette*.

I felt so lucky to have so many friends who **loved** me and were ready to help me!

Thea, Trap, Jim, and his sister, Ola, were there, as well as Bugsy Wugsy and Trappy, who were **wearing** jerseys for Turbo Cheese, Thea's team! We were also joined by Hope Goalfur and Chip Cross — the two **TEAM** captains — and the two coaches.

Finally, Hercule Poirat arrived, holding a banana in one paw and **waving** a Turbo Cheese flag with the other. He was a huge **FAN** of the team.

While I was busy greeting everyone,

Here's the Superfan Mega Pizza!

Trap **grabbed** the phone in my office and ordered a pizza (on my credit card, of course). He got the Superfan Mega Pizza: a giant triple-cheese pizza sprinkled with Parmesan and with a soccer-sized ball of mozzarella in the middle!

I moaned, "Isn't that going to be a bit heavy for lunch?"

He rolled his eyes. "Don't be the mold in the cheese, Cuz!"

Then Flora, *The Rodent's Gazette*'s expert in herbal medicines, spoke up. "After we have pizza, I'll make a nice **herbal tea** to help with digestion for anyone who wants it!"

While we munched on the pizza, we tried to come up with a plan.

"So, every strange accident at the Mighty Mice and Sewer Rats matches always ended up in their favor," Thea said. "Maybe they were the ones who caused the accidents!"

Chip added, "Yes, but there hasn't been any proof that they were responsible. That's why they haven't been disqualified."

"We have to catch them in the act!" Benjamin cried. "If we manage to surprise them while they're setting up their tricks, the IRFS can disqualify them."

"Bravo, Benjamin!" I cheered. "That's a great idea! But . . . how are we going to do that?"

Hercule CHUCKLED. "Geronimo, don't worry about it! I have here a gadget to peel those bad bananas! It's my special invention: the BANANACAM!"

And he pulled out a video camera shaped like a banana.

"Someone can film all the matches with this bananacam, so if the Mighty Mice or the Sewer Rats try any TRICKS, we'll have proof that they're cheating. We just need a volunteer!"

Trap chuckled and flicked my ear. "GERONIMO VOLUNTEERS!"

Hee, hee, hee!

He volunteers!

I . . . actually . . .

TAP

I sputtered, "Well, I . . . actually . . ."

But everyone cheered, "Bravo, Geronimo!"

I COULDN'T BACK OUT NOW!

Thea, Chip, and Hope got up to leave. "We're going to go get ready for the match tonight. Geronimo, FILM the games with the bananacam! We're counting on you!"

As they were leaving, Jim called, "Thea, good luck! I'll be cheering for you!"

Hercule squeaked, "And I'll be cheering

Bravo, Geronimo!

Hooray for my uncle!

Thank you, Geronimo!

for you, too, Thea! I'm your biggest fan!"

Jim scoffed. "No way! I'm her biggest fan!"

Hercule shouted, "NO, I AM!"

Then Bruce Hyena joined in, squeaking, "Actually, I'm her biggest fan! Didn't you know?"

While the three bickered, I took the bananacam and left the office. I'm her brother, so I know I'm her biggest fan!

As I walked, I got a brilliant id**e**a. I decided to go to the stadium early. If someone was trying to **sabotage** the matches, maybe they were doing so before the games even started!

Two Teams in Leopard Print

When I reached the stadium, I saw a **crowd** of reporters at the entrance.

They were all holding microphones toward Madame No, who had arrived in

Obviously, I want to win!

a leopard-print <u>stretch</u> limousine with dark windows.

Madame No got out of the car, wearing a **leopard-print** trench coat. All the reporters crowded around her shouting questions.

"*Madame No*, why did you suddenly decide to sponsor these two soccer teams?"

LEOPARD-PRINT PURSE

LEOPARD-PRINT SUNGLASSES

She rudely kept texting on her leopard-print **cell phone**, then rummaged in

LEOPARD-PRINT CELL PHONE

her leopard-print purse, took out a pair of leopard-print sunglasses, and squeaked, **"Obviously, because I want to win. Anytime, anywhere, in any way!"**

A reporter said, "Madame No, it seems as though whenever your teams play, their opponents are involved in **mysterious** accidents."

Madame No scoffed. **"Lies! Slander! Falsehoods!** My teams always win because they're better than all the others — and because they wear athletic clothes from the brand **BAD SPORT**!"

Madame No's bodyguards lifted up an

enormouse banner that read BUY CLOTHES FROM BAD SPORT! and the reporters began wildly snapping photos.

Satisfied, Madame No got back into her car, but before she left, she leaned out the window. "**May the best teams win . . . that is, my teams! Because** *Madame No* **plays to win, got it? Anytime, anywhere, in any way!**"

The car left with a screech.

The reporters then turned to me.

"Do you agree, Mr. Stilton?"

I shook my snout. "I believe that it matters how you play, not just if you win!"

The crowd murmured, "He's right! Geronimo Stilton is right!"

But I was already heading off, clutching the BANANACAM. I had an important assignment to complete!

I entered the stadium thanks to my press pass. The stadium staff was already preparing the field for the match.

I **LOOKED** around carefully to try to spot any suspicious movements. I **turned**, and **turned**, and **turned** all around but didn't see anything.

Exhausted, I decided to sit down on a bench to rest.

But when I tried to get up again, I was stuck! The bench had just been PAINTED, and I hadn't seen the sign.

Great Gouda! What a mess!

My friend **CHIP** rushed over and tried to help me up from the bench, but my pants were still sticking.

Chip shook his head. "There's only one

solution: you'll have to take off your pants!"

I couldn't believe it. **"HOLEY CHEESE! I NEED MY PANTS!"**

"I'll loan you a pair of my soccer shorts!" Chip offered.

I turned **RED** as a cheese rind with embarrassment. Then I slipped out of my pants, which were still stuck to the bench.

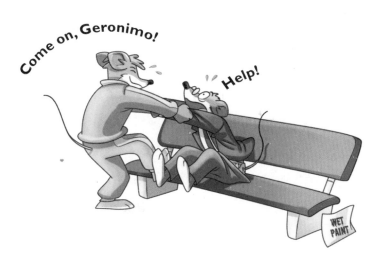

I was left standing in my underwear!

What a mess!

The Sewer Rats players pointed at me, snickering. "Stilton's in his underpants! What a cheesebrain!"

Reporters started snapping PHOTOS. "Can that blushing rodent really be Stilton, the famouse journalist? What was he doing on a bench with wet paint? And why is he in only his underwear? **What a scoop!**"

I escaped into the Squeakers' locker room and came back dressed in a pair of Chip's SOCCER SHORTS and my usual dress shirt and green suit jacket. I looked ridicumouse!

Chip tried to cheer me up. "Geronimo,

thank you for everything you're doing to help us. Good luck filming with the BANANACAM!"

I sighed. "Thanks. We can't just accuse the Mighty Mice and the Sewer Rats of **cheating** without proof."

"Don't worry! There are two matches tonight, and the first one hasn't even started yet. If they're setting up something **suspicious**, you'll have time to catch them in the act!"

LET THE GAME BEGIN!

The Super Cup was about to begin . . .

The stadium was full of **FANS** wearing the colors of their favorite teams. Banners were waving, and the crowd was already starting to cheer.

The Squeakers would play first against the Mighty Mice. The two teams shook 🐾🐾🐾🐾, and then the referee placed the ball at the center mark. The Squeakers were the home team, so the Mighty Mice had the ball first.

Jim Dribbles began commentating. "And . . . they're off!"

The Mighty Mice immediately went on offense, but as soon as they entered their

WHAT HAPPENS AT A SOCCER MATCH?

1. The two teams enter and shake paws.
2. The national anthem for each team is sung.
3. The game begins! The first half of play lasts forty-five minutes.
4. There's a fifteen-minute halftime break.
5. The second half of game play lasts another forty-five minutes, for a total game time of ninety minutes.
6. The referee can add stoppage time to the end of the match if play was interrupted by injuries or other delays.
7. If there's a tie at the end of the game, in direct elimination matches (such as tournaments), two extra fifteen-minute periods can be played.
8. If there's still a tie at the end of the extra time, it goes to penalty kicks: each team gets five kicks, and whoever scores the most wins the match.

opponents' territory, the Squeakers' defense intercepted the ball!

I wasn't watching the match, though. I was filming with the bananacam, panning around the field, ready to catch any **suspicious** behavior.

I was so focused that I didn't realize that the **BALL** had flown off the field . . . until it hit me right in the head!

Feeling dazed, I moved to the other side of

THEN IT HIT ME SQUARE UNDER MY TAIL!

Oof!

Ow!

THE BALL HIT ME RIGHT IN THE HEAD!

the **FIELD** . . . but the ball flew out of play again and hit me square under my tail!

I decided to move behind the Squeakers' **GOAL**. Then the Mighty Mice went back on offense, and their top scorer gave a powerful kick . . . which missed the goal but got me right on the snout! I fainted and flopped over like string cheese.

When I came to, one of the assistant referees was fanning me with his flag. The

WHO CAN GO ON THE SOCCER FIELD?

1. Each team's starting players and substitutes (who enter the game when there's a substitution)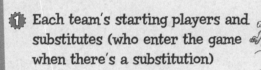

2.  The referee and the assistant referees, who ensure that the rules of the game are followed

3. The coaches, who lead the team in fitness, training, and game tactics

4. The athletic trainers, who help the players prepare for the game physically so that they don't get injured

5. The medical staff, who handles any injuries to the players

first half was almost over, and the score was 0–0.

I would have liked to sit and **WATCH** the match, but I had an important mission to complete: I needed to uncover the Mighty Mice's evil plan!

I didn't want to get hit by the ball again, so I decided to go check out the locker rooms. Maybe I'd find some **clues** there!

Everyone was out watching the game, and my pawsteps **echoed** in the deserted hallway.

The door to the Mighty Mice locker room was open.

Hmm . . . everything seemed to be in order . . .

I was about to go back outside when I heard different **PAWSTEPS** coming down the hall. Squeak! The first half was over, and the players were returning to the locker rooms to rest!

I hid in a dark **CORNER** of the hallway.

While the players passed by me, I heard them saying spitefully, "We still haven't scored a goal against those weaklings . . ."

"But we have the whole second half to show them up! **HA, HA, HAAA!**"

"Yeah, and we've got a few tricks up our

We haven't scored . . .

We'll do it soon!

With our little trick . . .

sleeves! HEE, HEE, HEEEEE!"

My whiskers shook with outrage. I wished I had been recording that with the bananacam. It sounded like those sneaky Mighty Mice really were going to cheat to win!

But there were more of them than there was of me, so I stayed **hidden** until halftime was over and the players had returned to the field. When they were all gone, I came out from my corner, and . . .

1. I tripped over a ball left on the ground . . .
2. Then I grabbed on to a locker door to keep from falling . . .
3. A flag by the locker fell and bonked me on the head . . .
4. Then I stepped on a wet towel and slid all the way into the Mighty Mice locker room!

The door closed behind me. **CLICK!**

I tried to leave, but the door was stuck. **I WAS LOCKED INSIDE!**

I grabbed the door, pulling with all my might. Just then someone on the other side flung it open . . .

AND IT WAS NOT A MOUSE I WAS EXPECTING TO SEE!

Youch!

4 I SLIPPED ON A WET TOWEL . . .

Oops!

3 A FLAG BONKED ME ON THE HEAD . . .

SWISHHHHHH

What are you doing here?

My whiskers shook with surprise. The mouse who opened the door was the referee, Sharp Foulfur!

"Excuse me, but aren't you Geronimo Stilton?" he said. "The editor of *The Rodent's Gazette*? What are you doing here?"

I tried to explain. "Um, yes, hello — I was in the hallway, then the ball — I mean, the flag, well, and the locker . . . anyway, I ended up **LOCKED** in here!" Then, playing it cool, I said, "Um, Mr. Sharp, I might as well ask, too — what are you doing here?"

He sputtered, "Um, I . . . I mean — actually, you could say . . . maybe, sort of . . . perhaps . . . well, important, SECRET referee duties! But now I have to go. The game is about to start again!"

He scurried off, looking guilty, and I followed him.

What "**SECRET** referee duties" could lead him to wander around the locker rooms?

And why the Mighty Mice **locker room** in particular?

HMM . . . HOW STRANGE!

Hmm . . . how strange!

I have to go!

IN THE FINAL MINUTE!

The Squeakers had control of the ball at the start of the second half. They quickly advanced it down the field.

Jim commentated, "And now the ball is being passed to Chip, who stops it with his chest and advances like lightning! He dodges **one** of the Mighty Mice players! He dodges **two**! He dodges **three**! He's in the penalty area! But . . . What's happening? It looks like an enormouse **COCKROACH** is on the field! Is that a robot? What's it doing there?! The robot cockroach is right between Chip's paws, and . . . it steals the ball!

"I've never seen anything like this before!"

All the Squeakers began to run after the **MECHANICAL** cockroach, which CROSSED the field in a flash and dropped the ball right in front of a Mighty Mouse.

I waited for the referee to call a foul, but he seemed to be distracted.

What's that?!

Jim was **shocked**. "An enormouse cockroach is on the field, but the referee doesn't seem to have seen it! **How strange!**"

The Mighty Mouse snickered and took the ball down the field. They were ready to go — almost as if they'd been expecting such a strange occurrence!

Meanwhile, the robot cockroach was skittering between the feet of the Squeakers players, making them trip and interrupting

Um...

Take that!

the game . . . but the referee was still busy writing!

I was so anxious I PUllED my whiskers tight. "Great Gorgonzola, watch out! The Mighty Mice are going to **score** a goal!"

The Mighty Mice forward charged to the goal with a **MIGHTY** kick. But the Squeakers' goalkeeper dove to the left and managed to stop the ball!

The whole stadium erupted in cheers.

Squeak!

Let's stop it!

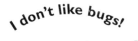
I don't like bugs!

Meanwhile, Chip managed to capture the robot cockroach, then passed it to me. "Take it, Geronimo!"

I turned as PALE as cottage cheese. I don't like bugs!

As I took hold of it, I heard a tiny voice coming from its metal antennae, giving the robot commands. "Are you listening?

"KEEP DISRUPTING THE SQUEAKERS!"

I barked into the transmitter, "I don't know who you are, but you should be ashamed of yourself for using these tricks! I'm taking this ROBOT to the tournament director."

The voice cried out, "We've been

discovered! Begin: **SELF-DESTRUCT**!"

The mechanical cockroach shook, made a sizzling sound, and shut off.

I stared at it in shock. Its **circuits** were fried! I couldn't give it to the **IRFS** as proof. And I was so distracted by the cockroach that I forgot to film anything!

Meanwhile, the second half of the match was almost over, and the score was still 0–0.

Then, in the final minute, when everyone had lost hope . . . Chip Cross got the ball!

Shame on you!

BRRR ZZZTTT!

SELF-DESTRUCT!

Jim was excited. "We're in stoppage time, but Chip isn't stopping — he's taking the **BALL**! He heads toward the Mighty Mice side of the field! Time is almost up! He crosses the center line! The referee is about to whistle — but what is Chip doing? He's shooting? The ball soars across the whole half of the field and . . . INCREDIBLE!

INCREDIBLE! INCREDIBLE! INCREDIBLE!

Goooooooooaaaaaaaaal!
Goooooooooaaaaaaaaal!
Goooooooooaaaaaaaaaal!

"The goalkeeper didn't think the ball could make it from so far away, but **CHIP** has done it! What a champion! The Squeakers win the Super Cup!"

The crowd cheered, *"Squeakers! Squeakers! Squeakers!"*

It was the most beautiful goal I'd ever seen! And one of my favorite teams had won! What an ending to the game!

It's Not Time to Celebrate Yet!

The Squeakers left the field carrying Chip on their shoulders in triumph, bathing in the cheers of their fans.

I wanted to **CELEBRATE** their victory, but it wasn't the right time yet.

Hooray! Way to go! Hooray!

The match between Turbo Cheese and the Sewer Rats was coming up next, and I still needed to find proof that Madame No was up to her tricks again!

Pssst ...
pssst ...

As the players came on to the field to warm up, I noticed Sharp Foulfur on the touchline, **muttering** on his phone.

I heard him say: "Yes, I'm sorry they won . . . **pssst** . . . but I couldn't stop it . . . **pssst pssst** . . . I can't talk now . . . **pssst pssst pssst** . . . it's too risky!"

Before I could get closer, he ended the call.

HMM . . . HOW STRANGE!

I went over to the Turbo Cheese bench as the team warmed up.

THE SOCCER PLAYER'S WARM-UP

Hup, hup ...

1 Start with a light jog. Run slowly at first, then speed up!

...nine, ten!

2 For your first stretch, balance on one leg and pull the other foot back until it touches your tail, holding it for ten seconds. Then switch legs.

Just like this!

3 With feet together and legs straight, bend over and touch your toes. Hold that position for ten seconds, then slowly return to a standing position.

A good stretch!

4 Next is a lunge. Bend your front leg (with your foot flat on the ground) and keep your back leg straight. Hold the position for ten seconds, then switch legs.

Oooh ... aah!

5 Then, sitting on the ground, stretch your legs in a V-shape. Try to touch one foot with both paws, holding the position for ten seconds. Then switch legs.

Stretch it out!

6 Finally, still seated on the ground but with your legs both straight ahead, try to touch your toes without bending your knees, and hold that position for ten seconds. Then slowly return to an upright position.

Thea saw me coming. "Well, Geronimo, any news? Did you learn anything? Did you get anything on the bananacam?"

I shook my snout. "Not yet. But I'm keeping my EYES open. If you ask me, though, the referee is acting very strangely . . ."

Thea gasped. "What are you talking about, Geronimo? Sharp Foulfur is the best, most honest, most famous referee on all of Mouse Island! He would never cheat or work for Madame No."

I wasn't so convinced. "Well, something doesn't add up . . ."

Hope Goalfur interrupted us. "The match is about to begin! Let's go, Thea!"

I gave her a hug. "Break a paw! I'll be cheering for you!"

The referee whistled for the game to

start, and Turbo Cheese and the Sewer Rats started playing! I held up the bananacam.

However, things soon took a **suspicious** turn.

In the tenth minute, while one of the Sewer Rats was dribbling, the **BALL** went out of bounds for a moment — but the referee was on the other side of the field and didn't notice.

Jim gasped. "**How strange!** The referee didn't notice that the ball went out of play! Anyway, the match goes on . . ."

Scratch Scratch Scratch

In the twentieth minute, one of the Sewer Rats' **forwards** was offside — but Sharp was *scratching* his snout and didn't notice.

Jim couldn't believe it.

"Whaaaat?! The referee was scratching his snout and didn't see that she was **offside**! Now the Sewer Rats player tries to score . . . but Hope Goalfur blocks it! **WAY TO GO!**"

In the thirtieth minute, Thea took the ball and ran toward the goal. But when she tried to score, one of the Sewer Rats players grabbed her JERSEY, making her lose her balance, and she missed her shot!

The referee, however, was apparently distracted by a butterfly and didn't see a thing. He didn't whistle the foul or penalize the Sewer Rats player.

A butterfly!

Jim was stupefied. "**Come onnnn!** It's unbelievable, my dear mice! A clear violation by one of the Sewer Rats, but the referee didn't see anything! He was watching a butterfly! I can't believe it!"

In the fortieth minute, the Sewer Rats were on offense in Turbo Cheese territory. Without any other mice near her, one of the Sewer Rats fell to the ground, grabbing her leg and shouting, "OW! OW! OW!"

The Turbo Cheese players threw their paws up. "We didn't do anything! We didn't touch her! **She's faking!**"

But the referee was bending down to tie his shoe and hadn't seen what happened.

When he got to his feet, he whistled and said, "Foul by Turbo Cheese in their own territory! **FREE KICK!**"

Jim was exasperated. "You can't be serious?! The Sewer Rats player wasn't hurt, she was **faking**! No one touched her! No one else was even near her — we all saw

it! All except the referee, who was too busy **TYING** his shoe! Holey cheese, it's unbelievable! He hadn't been paying any attention to the game at all."

The captain of the Sewer Rats smiled as Foulfur placed the ball on the penalty spot, then **RAN** up to it and kicked.

The ball flew toward the goal, right under the crossbar. Hope tried to **BLOCK** it. Unfortunately, she missed it by a whisker! The Sewer Rats had scored.

Jim shouted,

"Goooooooooooaaaaaaaaaal!"
"Goooooooooooaaaaaaaaaal!"
"Goooooooooooaaaaaaaaaal!"

A few seconds later, the referee whistled for the end of the first half.

Turbo Cheese returned to their locker room, ears drooping. Their morale was at rock bottom.

Caught You, Cheddarbreath!

I, however, had no intention of giving up!

I was convinced that something **suspicious** was going on, and that the referee, Sharp Foulfur, was involved.

I saw him skulking in a stadium hallway. He stopped in a dark corner.

I followed him, filming with the BANANACAM.

Sharp pulled out his phone and murmured, "Hello? Madame No? It's me!"

My whiskers trembled with outrage. He and Madame No really were working together! **WHAT A DISGRACE!**

The referee whispered, "Yes, I did just as you ordered, *Madame No*! I did my best not to see any of the Sewer Rats' FOULS, and I even managed to award them a **FREE KICK**! Thanks to me, the Sewer Rats are now in the lead . . . What did you say, Madame No? I can't hear you . . . No, I can't hear you! This **MASK** muffles sounds. Wait while I take it off . . ."

Then Sharp Foulfur looked around to be sure he was alone.

Hello? Madame No?

I hid myself better around the corner. Then . . . he took off his mask, and I saw that . . . Sharp . . .

WASN'T SHARP!

So that's why the referee wasn't acting right . . . IT WASN'T REALLY HIM!

Beneath the mask was **THE SHADOW**,

the most famouse thief on Mouse Island!

I **JUMPED** out of my hiding place, still **FILMING** with the bananacam. I squeaked, "I've caught you, cheddarbreath! **GO ON, CONFESS!** Where have you hidden the real referee?"

THE SHADOW'S eyes widened in surprise. "Geronimo Stilton? Squeeeeak!"

Then she ran away in a **FLASH**. I tried to run after her, but alas, I'm not really a sportsmouse!

After a few feet, I was out of breath!

And when I turned the corner, the Shadow had disappeared. But I had gotten BANANACAM footage of her: now I had proof that Madame No had **sabotaged** the matches to make sure her teams won!

I returned to the field to warn Thea. Halftime was almost over, and Turbo Cheese were getting ready to play again.

I shouted, "Thea! I have **shocking** news! You're never going to believe what I just saw. The referee isn't Sharp — it's the

The Shadow

The Shadow is the most famouse thief on Mouse Island — which is why Madame No has chosen her as her number-one associate.

Shadow! She was wearing a mask and pretending to be him!"

Hope gasped. "Wait, then what happened to the real referee?"

At that moment a basket of soccer balls nearby started to shake, and we heard someone moan "MMMPh! MMMPh! MMMPh!"

Mmmph ...

We pulled the balls out of the basket, and at the bottom we found the real Sharp Foulfur, TIED UP and gagged!

"Thank you for saving me, friends!" he cried as I helped him climb out. "While I was trapped, I could hear the sportscast — I'm outraged that someone took my place as referee to give an unfair advantage to the Sewer Rats!

"BUT NOW tHat I'M free, I'LL Be tHe ONe CaLLiNG tHe FOULS!"

He ran off, *BLOWING* on his whistle.

Go, Turbo Cheese!

Just then I received a text message from Jim Dribbles.

CHEESE NIBLETS! WHAT COULD HAVE HAPPENED?

I reached the commentator's booth and found Jim Dribbles seated in a corner

Geronimo, please run up to the commentator's booth as soon as possible! It's an emergency!

with his snout down. He was grasping the *microphone* and had tears in his eyes.

"Jim! What's wrong?" I squeaked.

He took out a notebook and wrote: *I shouted so loudly during the first half that I lost my voice! Now*

what am I going to do?

Then he burst into tears!

I tried to console him. "Don't worry, Jim, we'll find a solution. I'm calling Flora — she'll make a super-healing herbal tea for you. Your voice will come back right away!"

Jim wrote, *There's no time — the second half is about to start! Only you can save me, Geronimo. I'm begging you: Please do the commentating for me!*

"Okay, Jim! I won't let you down!" I agreed. "There's just, um, a little problem. I'm not exactly an expert when it comes to the rules of soccer."

Jim immediately opened up his backpack and pulled out an **ENORMOUSE**, well-used manual called:

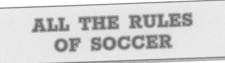

ALL THE RULES OF SOCCER

It was a book given to him by his grandfather, who had inscribed it, *To my dear grandson, Jim Dribbles, star commentator! Love, your grandfather Penalty Dribbles.*

Just then the second half of the match started! Leafing frantically through the manual, I began to commentate, doing my **best** (or maybe my **worst**?). "Um, here's Turbo Cheese on offense! They pass to the **RiGHt** . . . no, to the **LEFt**! Careful, there, that's a **FOUL** . . . er, actually, just a dribble! Wait, what is that? Is that the penalty area? Cheese on a stick!"

It was so stressful! My anxiety about sportscasting made me even more confused than usual!

Flora had arrived with the herbal tea, and Jim was **drinking** it as he pulled on his FUR anxiously. Flora cheered, *"You can do it, Thea! Go, Turbo Cheese!"*

She passes to the right . . .
No, the left!

I continued my commentary. "And now my sister, um, I mean, forward Thea Stilton intercepts a defensive pass from the Sewer Rats. Thea passes to her teammate, who moves in a SQUARE — I mean, a TRIANGLE — and passes it again, up high, to Thea, with a criss — I mean, a cross!

"THEA HEADS THE BALL . . . AND IT'S A GOOOOAAAAL!

Goooooooooaaaaaal!
Gooooooooaaaaaal!
Goooooooaaaaaal!

"Turbo Cheese has **TIED** the game! Hooray! Um, I mean . . . well done, everyone — to you, too, Sewer Rats!"

The match remained a tie right up to the end of the ninety minutes. No one scored during the five minutes of stoppage time, and then even during the thirty minutes of extra time, the score stayed tied. It was time for **PENALTY KICKS**.

Each team would have five opportunities to score a goal, and whoever scored the most would be the winner!

The mice chosen to kick were all the best players, and one by one, they each scored.

Finally, it came down to the final kick for the Sewer Rats. If they missed, Turbo Cheese would win the championship.

Hope was in the goal, super focused and ready to jump.

The top scorer for the Sewer Rats struck the ball. It was a beautiful kick, headed right for the crossbar . . . But Hope leaped like a grasshopper and grabbed the ball firmly with both paws!

The entire stadium erupted in cheers.

I grabbed the microphone, and Jim, who suddenly found his voice, shouted along with me: *"Turbo Cheese has won the Super Cup!"*

Both teams shook paws as friends.

Then the CAPTAINS of both of the day's winning teams lifted their trophies up, to the cheers of their fans!

THE MOUSE ISLAND SUPER CUP FINALS!
Blocked!
The Sewer Rats' top scorer launched a beautiful kick, but Hope Goalfur managed to block it!
Hooray!
Yay!
The stadium erupted in cheers for Turbo Cheese!
Hooray!
The captains of the Squeakers and Turbo Cheese lifted their cups, to the cheering of their fans!

THE TRUE SPIRIT OF SOCCER

Every sports news outlet covered the scandal of the sabotaged matches. The story was in the paper for weeks and Madame No had gone into hiding to avoid all the angry fans. The Mighty Mice and the Sewer Rats were banned from the IRFS and disbanded for good!

The weekend after the Super Cup, I organized a big PICNIC at the Stilton family farm to celebrate the wins. I invited all my friends, the whole Stilton family, and the Squeakers and Turbo Cheese players. Every mouse brought something to eat that they'd made with their own PAWS, and we had lunch in an enormouse meadow.

MOUSPORT

Unmasking Madame No's Foul Play

Thanks to the contributions of a fan who prefers to remain anonymous, there is now proof that the games played by the Mighty Mice and the Sewer Rats during the Super Cup tournament were fixed in their favor. The two teams were banned by the IRFS and disbanded for good.

The sponsor of the Mighty Mice and the Sewer Rats, the famouse Madame No, has commented, "I deny everything! I didn't do anything! And what does it matter if my teams are disbanded? I've never even liked soccer, so there!"

After lunch, everyone helped **clean up** the area so that it was left as beautiful as we'd found it.

While the mice **PLAYED** and **chattered**, I sat inside, peacefully munching on cheese and reading a book. Can you guess what it was?

It was **ALL THE RULES OF SOCCER**, the manual that Jim had loaned me!

Benjamin, Bugsy, and Trappy were all with me. Together, we **STUDIED** the rules so we could better appreciate soccer games.

Then Trappy said, "Uncle Geronimo, Thea is organizing a soccer game right now! **LET'S GO PLAY, TOO!**"

"But it's getting a little chilly out and I just got comfortable on my couch!" I tried to protest.

"Please, Uncle G?" Benjamin asked. I

could never say no to my favorite nephew! I smiled. "Sounds fun — I'll play! The field is just over there!"

We formed TEAMS that each had a mix of adult and young mice, and began to play a super soccer game all together.

The match was refereed by Sharp Foulfur. He'd been invited to the picnic along with the players!

Even though it was cold, and I'm not exactly a sportsmouse, I gave it my best shot, and had a wonderful time.

We weren't playing to win — just to be together. And that, my dear rodent friends, is the true spirit of soccer: playing to have fun, playing fairly, respecting the rules, and respecting one another!

Because the real trophies aren't shining cups won in big matches,

but rather the good memories we make by **PLAYING** with respect and loyalty — memories that we'll always keep with us, in our hearts!

And that's the truth, or my name isn't *Geronimo Stilton*!

Rodent's honor!

PLAYING FIELD: The surface must be green. The dimensions must be 110–120 yards (100–110 meters) by 70–80 yards (64–75 meters). The longer boundary lines are called touchlines, and the shorter lines are called goal lines. In each corner of the field, there must be a pole with a flag. The goals must be made of posts that are 8 yards (7.32 meters) apart and connected by a crossbar that's 8 feet (2.44 meters) high. The goalposts and crossbar must be white.

BALL: The ball must be spherical, made of leather or synthetic leather, with a 27–28 inch (68–70 centimeter) circumference, and weigh 14–16 ounces (410–450 grams).

NUMBER OF PLAYERS: Each team must be made up of no more than eleven players, one of whom is the goalkeeper. A team cannot play with fewer than seven players.

REFEREE: Each match must be regulated by a referee, whose job is to make sure the rules of the game are followed.

ASSISTANT REFEREES: Two assistant referees signal to the referee when the ball goes out of play or offside, and when fouls happen outside the referee's view.

GAME DURATION: The game consists of two halves that are forty-five minutes each, with a fifteen-minute halftime in between.

START OF PLAY: The game starts or restarts with a kickoff from the center line at the beginning of each half and after a goal.

BALL OUT OF PLAY: The ball is no longer in play when the entire ball goes past the touchlines or the goal lines, or when the referee has stopped play.

SCORING A GOAL: A goal is scored when the ball goes past the goal line between the goalposts and under the crossbar.

OFFSIDE: A player is offside when, in the moment when a teammate passes them the ball, they are closer to their opponent's goal line than both the ball and at least two players of the opposing team.

FOULS: Fouls are called for any violent conduct or if a player touches the ball with their hands (other than the goalkeeper in the penalty area).

FREE KICK: When a team fouls, a free kick is awarded to the opposing team. It is taken from the place where the foul occurred.

PENALTY KICK: When a team fouls inside their penalty area, a penalty kick is awarded to the opposing team. It is taken from the penalty mark.

THROW-IN: After the ball goes out of play, a throw-in can restart play. A player uses their hands to throw it in, but a goal cannot be scored directly from a throw-in.

GOAL KICK: If the ball goes out of play over the goal line and the last player to touch it was on the opposing team, the ball is kicked back in play from the goal line.

CORNER KICK: If the ball goes out of play over the goal line and the last player to touch it was on the defending team, the ball is kicked back into play from a corner of the field. Opponents must remain at least 10 yards (9.15 meters) away.

THE WINNING TEAM: The team that scores the most goals is the winner!

ASSIST: a pass that results in a goal (from the player it was passed to).

BACKHEEL: a kick of the ball backward with the heel.

BALL CARRIER: the player who has possession of the ball.

BENCH: the area on the sides of the field where the technical staff and the substitute players spend the match.

BICYCLE KICK: an acrobatic strike where a player kicks the ball in midair so it goes backward over their head.

BREAK: when players quickly advance the ball down the field toward the opponent's goal before the defenders can get there. Also called advantage.

CAPTAIN: a player who's a leader on the team. They wear an armband during the game, participate in the coin toss before kickoff, and can help with communication between the referee and the team.

CAUTION: a warning to a player who has committed a foul, signaled by the referee with a yellow card. If the player receives a second yellow card, it's equivalent to a red card.

COACH: one who trains the players.

CORNER KICK: see The Basic Rules of Soccer (page 102–103).

CROSS: a long pass from a player near the side of the field to a player near the opponent's goal.

CROSSBAR: the highest part of the goal, which is parallel to the ground.

DEAD BALL: a situation where the ball is not in play.

DEFENDER: a defensive player, who tries to prevent the other team from scoring.

DEFENSE: when a team protects their own territory against the other team's possession of the ball.

DERBY: a match between two rival teams from the same area.

DRIBBLING: moving the ball carefully forward by closely controlling it with the feet.

EXTRA TIME: if there must be a winning team and the result at the end of regulation time is a tie, two extra periods of fifteen minutes each are played. If the situation doesn't change, it goes to penalty kicks.

FEINT: a movement to try to confuse or trick an opponent, so they think the ball will go in a different direction.

FORMATION: how the players are positioned on the field.

FORWARD: an offensive player whose job is to score goals. Also known as a striker.

FOUL: an action by a player that is deemed a violation by the referee, resulting in a free kick or penalty kick for the opposing team.

FREE KICK: see The Basic Rules of Soccer (page 102–103).

GOAL: the area that the ball must enter to earn a point. Also the name of the point awarded.

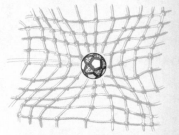

GOALKEEPER: the player who protects the goal, and the only player who can use their hands on the ball (only while in the penalty area).

HEADER: a shot or pass of the ball made by the head.

INTERCEPTION: a quick change in possession of the ball, when play turns from defense to offense.

LINESMEN: two assistant referees who follow the match from the touchlines. They help the referee by signaling offsides and substitutions. Their role is critical when a foul is committed outside the referee's field of vision.

LOB: an upward kick that passes the ball high in the air above an opponent without letting them intercept it. Also known as a chip or lofted pass.

MIDFIELDER: a player positioned in the center of the field who provides a link between the team's offense and defense.

NUTMEG: getting the ball past an opponent by passing it through their legs.

OFFENSE: when a team has possession of the ball and plays to try to score a goal. Also called attacking.

OFFSIDE: see The Basic Rules of Soccer (page 102–103).

Own goal!

OWN GOAL: when the ball is deflected or kicked unintentionally by a team into their own goal, giving the other team a point.

PASS: a kick or strike of the ball with the feet, leg, head, or chest that sends it toward a teammate.

PENALTY AREA: a rectangular area of the field in front of each goal, inside which the goalkeeper can use their hands on the ball.

PENALTY KICK: see The Basic Rules of Soccer (page 102–103).

RED CARD: what the referee raises to signal a serious violation has been committed. A player who gets a red card is immediately expelled from the game and their position cannot be replaced.

REGULATION TIME: two halves of forty-five minutes each, plus stoppage time.

SUBSTITUTE: a player on the bench who may replace another player on the field in a match.

TACKLE: an action to steal the ball from an opponent.

TOP SCORER: a player who scores a lot of goals.

WALL: a formation of players from one team (in a line) to defend their own goal when the opposing team has a free kick.

WINGER: a player who plays on one side of the field. Their job is to pass the ball to the forwards. Historically called an outside position.

YELLOW CARD: what the referee raises to signal a caution.

Chip Cross

The top scorer in New Mouse City!

See you at the next match!

Don't miss a single fabumouse adventure!

Up Next:

You've never seen Geronimo Stilton like this before!

Get your paws on the all-new

Geronimo Stilton

graphic novels. You've gouda* have them!

*Gouda is a type of cheese.

Don't miss any of my adventures in the Kingdom of Fantasy!

THE KINGDOM OF FANTASY

THE QUEST FOR PARADISE: THE RETURN TO THE KINGDOM OF FANTASY

THE AMAZING VOYAGE: THE THIRD ADVENTURE IN THE KINGDOM OF FANTASY

THE DRAGON PROPHECY: THE FOURTH ADVENTURE IN THE KINGDOM OF FANTASY

THE VOLCANO OF FIRE: THE FIFTH ADVENTURE IN THE KINGDOM OF FANTASY

THE SEARCH FOR TREASURE: THE SIXTH ADVENTURE IN THE KINGDOM OF FANTASY

THE ENCHANTED CHARMS: THE SEVENTH ADVENTURE IN THE KINGDOM OF FANTASY

THE PHOENIX OF DESTINY: AN EPIC KINGDOM OF FANTASY ADVENTURE

THE HOUR OF MAGIC: THE EIGHTH ADVENTURE IN THE KINGDOM OF FANTASY

THE WIZARD'S WAND: THE NINTH ADVENTURE IN THE KINGDOM OF FANTASY

THE SHIP OF SECRETS: THE TENTH ADVENTURE IN THE KINGDOM OF FANTASY

THE DRAGON OF FORTUNE: AN EPIC KINGDOM OF FANTASY ADVENTURE

THE GUARDIAN OF THE REALM: THE ELEVENTH ADVENTURE IN THE KINGDOM OF FANTASY

THE ISLAND OF DRAGONS: THE TWELFTH ADVENTURE IN THE KINGDOM OF FANTASY

THE BATTLE FOR THE CRYSTAL CASTLE: THE THIRTEENTH ADVENTURE IN THE KINGDOM OF FANTASY

THE KEEPERS OF THE EMPIRE: THE FOURTEENTH ADVENTURE IN THE KINGDOM OF FANTASY

Thea Stilton

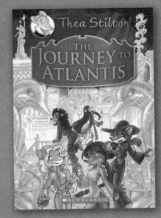

Secret Fairies

Don't miss any of these exciting series featuring the Thea Sisters!

Treasure Seekers

Mouseford Academy

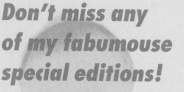

Don't miss any of my fabumouse special editions!

THE JOURNEY
TO ATLANTIS

THE SECRET OF
THE FAIRIES

THE SECRET OF
THE SNOW

THE CLOUD
CASTLE

THE TREASURE
OF THE SEA

THE LAND OF
FLOWERS

THE SECRET OF
THE CRYSTAL
FAIRIES

THE DANCE OF
THE STAR FAIRIES

THE MAGIC OF
THE MIRROR

Don't miss any of these exciting Thea Sisters adventures!

Thea Stilton and the Dragon's Code

Thea Stilton and the Mountain of Fire

Thea Stilton and the Ghost of the Shipwreck

Thea Stilton and the Secret City

Thea Stilton and the Mystery in Paris

Thea Stilton and the Cherry Blossom Adventure

Thea Stilton and the Star Castaways

Thea Stilton: Big Trouble in the Big Apple

Thea Stilton and the Ice Treasure

Thea Stilton and the Secret of the Old Castle

Thea Stilton and the Blue Scarab Hunt

Thea Stilton and the Prince's Emerald

Thea Stilton and the Mystery on the Orient Express

Thea Stilton and the Dancing Shadows

Thea Stilton and the Legend of the Fire Flowers

Thea Stilton and the Spanish Dance Mission

**Thea Stilton and the
Journey to the Lion's Den**

**Thea Stilton and the
Great Tulip Heist**

**Thea Stilton and the
Chocolate Sabotage**

**Thea Stilton and the
Missing Myth**

**Thea Stilton and the
Lost Letters**

**Thea Stilton and the
Tropical Treasure**

**Thea Stilton and the
Hollywood Hoax**

**Thea Stilton and the
Madagascar Madness**

**Thea Stilton and the
Frozen Fiasco**

**Thea Stilton and the
Venice Masquerade**

**Thea Stilton and the
Niagara Splash**

**Thea Stilton and the
Riddle of the Ruins**

**Thea Stilton and the
Phantom of the Orchestra**

**Thea Stilton and the
Black Forest Burglary**

**Thea Stilton and the
Race for the Gold**

**Thea Stilton and the
Rainforest Rescue**

**Thea Stilton and the
American Dream**

**Thea Stilton and the
Roman Holiday**

**Thea Stilton and the
Fiesta in Mexico**

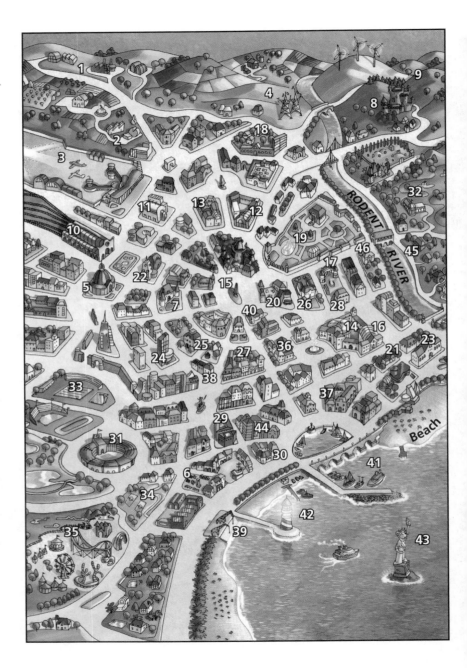

Map of New Mouse City

1. Industrial Zone
2. Cheese Factories
3. Angorat International Airport
4. WRAT Radio and Television Station
5. Cheese Market
6. Fish Market
7. Town Hall
8. Snotnose Castle
9. The Seven Hills of Mouse Island
10. Mouse Central Station
11. Trade Center
12. Movie Theater
13. Gym
14. Catnegie Hall
15. Singing Stone Plaza
16. The Gouda Theater
17. Grand Hotel
18. Mouse General Hospital
19. Botanical Gardens
20. Cheap Junk for Less (Trap's store)
21. Aunt Sweetfur and Benjamin's House
22. Museum of Modern Art
23. University and Library
24. *The Daily Rat*
25. *The Rodent's Gazette*
26. Trap's House
27. Fashion District
28. The Mouse House Restaurant
29. Environmental Protection Center
30. Harbor Office
31. Mousidon Square Garden
32. Golf Course
33. Swimming Pool
34. Tennis Courts
35. Curlyfur Island Amousement Park
36. Geronimo's House
37. Historic District
38. Public Library
39. Shipyard
40. Thea's House
41. New Mouse Harbor
42. Luna Lighthouse
43. The Statue of Liberty
44. Hercule Poirat's Office
45. Petunia Pretty Paws's House
46. Grandfather William's House

Map of Mouse Island

Dear mouse friends,
Thanks for reading, and farewell
till the next book.
It'll be another whisker-licking-good
adventure, and that's a promise!

Geronimo Stilton